# Town Teddy & Country Bear

TOUR THE
USA

To Brooke Simmons,

STARS & STRIPES
FUR-EVER!

2016

For my children Lisa and Cory,
may you always find pleasure
in the beauty of
America's national treasures
–K.B.

First edition/First printing
Copyright ©2008 Kathleen Bart

To purchase additional copies of this book, please contact:
Reverie Publishing Company
130 Wineow Street, Cumberland, Maryland 21502
888-721-4999
www.reveriepublishing.com

Library of Congress Control Number 2007937739
ISBN 978-1-932485-50-9

Printed and bound in Korea

# Town Teddy & Country Bear Tour the USA

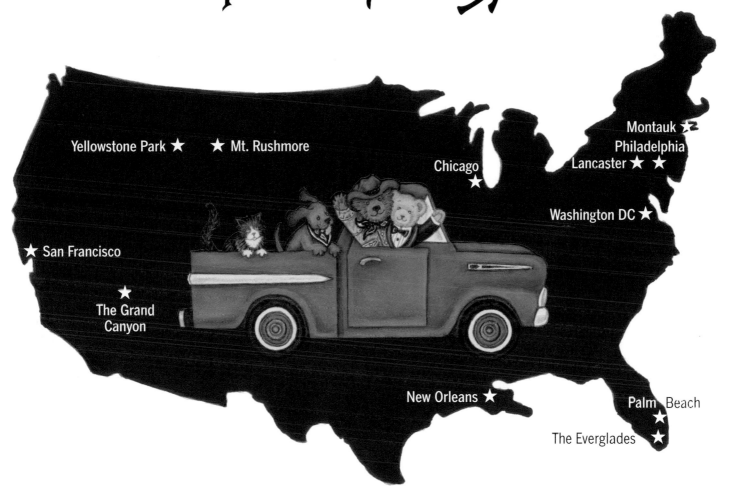

Yellowstone Park ★   ★ Mt. Rushmore

Montauk ★
Philadelphia
Lancaster ★ ★

Chicago ★

★ San Francisco

Washington DC ★

★
The Grand
Canyon

New Orleans ★

Palm Beach
★
The Everglades ★

## Written and Illustrated by
## Kathleen Bart

Reverie
PUBLISHING COMPANY

"I need a vacation!" Bandanna Bear sighed. "Sure, I love my quiet country life in Wyoming. But the good ol' USA has so many national parks and natural wonders to explore. Majestic mountains to climb. Rugged trails to hike. Peaceful places to camp. Yup, a camping trip will be a perfect vacation. And I know the best buddy to join me—my city cousin Tuxedo Teddy. Some fresh air and sunshine will do him good!"

"I need a holiday!" Tuxedo Teddy declared. "Sure, I love my busy city life in New York. But America has so many historic cities and national landmarks to tour. Spectacular sights to see. Magnificent museums to browse. Ritzy resorts to stay in. Yes, a first-class city tour will be a fabulous holiday! And I know the ideal travel companion— my country cousin Bandanna Bear. He could use a little culture and refinement!"

It didn't take Bandanna long to stuff his gear into his duffle bag. "I won't be fenced in by schedules. I'll just go where the spirit moves me. Yee haa!" His neighbor Bubba rumbled up in his red truck and honked. Bandanna tossed his duffle bag, tent and sleeping bag into the back of the truck and climbed in. Bandanna headed for the airport, leaving a trail of dust behind him.

Tuxedo spent all night planning his tour. "I'll have to stick to a tight schedule to take in all the sights I want to see!" He carefully folded his clothes into his set of matching designer luggage. The doorman loaded his luggage into the waiting limousine. Tuxedo glided to the airport in style.

The cousins met in the middle of the Golden Gate Bridge
in San Francisco and gave each other a great big bear hug.
Standing side by side, Tuxedo and Bandanna peered over
the bridge and gazed in wonder at the surrounding view.

Tuxedo interrupted their reverie. "Let's dip our paws into
the Pacific Ocean to mark the beginning of our tour. Then
we'll head east and end our trip by plunging our paws
into the Atlantic. Here's to exploring America the beautiful
from sea to shining sea!"

"To a great trip and a great friendship!" Bandanna added.

Tuxedo suggested celebrating the start of their tour with a lobster dinner on Fisherman's Wharf. Bandanna would have preferred to grab an egg roll in the streets of Chinatown, but he didn't want to disappoint Tuxedo. The tiny tidbits of lobster barely took the edge off of his hearty appetite. He filled up his growling belly with all the sourdough bread on the table.

That night, they checked into the swanky suite Tuxedo had reserved at a fancy hotel. Bandanna felt smothered as he sank into the soft bed. He couldn't sleep a wink. Finally, he tossed his sleeping bag on the floor, rolled it open and crawled inside. "Ahh, that's better!" He fell asleep dreaming of what he hoped to see the next day: rugged mountains carved with the faces of our most famous American Presidents.

Early the next morning, Bandanna threw open the drapes. "Wake up, Tux! We're leaving for Mount Rushmore." Tuxedo pulled the covers over his head. "But what about my schedule?" he mumbled. Bandanna pulled on Tuxedo's paw. "We're on vacation, not a business trip. Let's go!" Tuxedo was in no shape to argue, so he crawled into the truck that Bandanna had rented. "Wake me when we get there," he yawned.

A loud "thump, thump, thump!" woke Tuxedo. Bandanna jumped out to take a look. "Looks like we've got a flat tire! We'll have to hike the rest of the way." Tuxedo pointed to the presidents' faces carved in the distant mountain. "But Mount Rushmore must be a million miles away!"

"Nah. It's just a mile or two down the road. Trust me," Bandanna insisted.

The cousins started down the dirt road. The more they walked, the farther away the presidents' faces seemed to be. Tuxedo complained every step of the way. "I have blisters on my paws! I need a band aid! I need antibiotic ointment! Get me the first aid kit!"

They finally arrived at the stately sixty-foot stone faces of George Washington, Thomas Jefferson, Theodore Roosevelt and Abraham Lincoln. Tuxedo enjoyed the historical lecture by the Park Ranger. "Stay and listen while I get a closer view," Bandanna whispered. Then he climbed up Teddy Roosevelt's face, balanced on his mustache and waved.

"Get down from there at once!" the Park Ranger scolded. He drove Tuxedo and Bandanna back to their truck, fixed their flat and sent them on their way. "Now stay out of trouble and don't come back!"

"Now what?" Tuxedo scowled. "No worries!" replied Bandanna. "Let's drive to a national park to watch a famous geyser named Old Faithful erupt. With a name like that, what could possibly go wrong?"

"Are we there yet?" Tuxedo nagged.
"Admit it, Bandanna. You're lost."

"I'm not lost, I'm just taking the scenic route."
Suddenly they spotted a sign: *Welcome to Yellow-stone National Park*. "Told you so!" Bandanna smirked.

Wildlife stirred in the morning mist. Elk grazed in meadows, moose waded in ponds and eagles soared above waterfalls. Tuxedo was shocked to see animals roaming free. "The only wild animals I've ever seen were in the Central Park Zoo!"

At last, Bandanna and Tuxedo found Old Faithful. Tuxedo tapped his foot while he waited and waited for it to erupt. "This is as exciting as watching water come to a boil!" he growled. Finally, steam sputtered from Old Faithful. Within minutes, the geyser worked itself into a frenzy, gushing steamy water high into the sky.

Dreaming of a cozy bed by a fire-
place, Tuxedo hoped to stay at the
Old Faithful Lodge. But Bandanna
insisted on roughing it. "We'll sleep
out under the stars."

Tuxedo sat and sulked while Bandanna set
up his tent in the forest. When Bandanna
cooked over the campfire, Tuxedo complained
that the smoke stung his eyes. After dinner, he
demanded, "So where's the bathroom?"
Bandanna pointed to the woods. Tuxedo shud-
dered. "That's what *real* bears do," Bandanna
insisted.

Tuxedo spent the night shivering in his sleeping
bag while Bandanna snored like a cub. "This is
definitely *not* my idea of a holiday. Tomorrow,
we're going to do things *my* way," he vowed.

OLD
FAITHFUL
GEYSER

But Bandanna woke up early and took charge once again. The next thing Tuxedo knew, he was on on the back of a mule, riding through the Grand Canyon. The layered rock of the canyon glowed chili-pepper red in the Arizona sun.

The narrow and winding trail was like a spiral staircase, plunging one mile down into the depths of the canyon. Each time his mule stumbled over a rock, Tuxedo gasped. "You know I'm afraid of heights!"

"Take it easy! They've been taking mules down the canyon for a hundred years and they haven't lost anyone yet," Bandanna reassured him.

"There's a first time for everything," Tuxedo insisted. As if to prove his point, Tuxedo's mule broke into a trot. Each time his behind slapped the saddle he yelped, "Ouch! Ouch! Ouch!"

When the ride was over, a bow-legged Tuxedo limped away, rubbing his aching bottom. Furious over everything Bandanna had forced him to endure, Tuxedo threw a temper tantrum. "This is vacation, not boot camp!! Exhausting hikes, uncomfortable camping trips and grueling mule rides are *not* my cup of tea! I need indoor plumbing, a comfortable bed, and a decent latté! I've had it! Tomorrow I'm taking over. We're going to a city by a lovely lake to enjoy the finer things in life. This time it's my way or the highway!"

BRIGHT ANGEL TRAIL

RIM TRAIL

When Bandanna awoke the next morning, Tuxedo had already swapped their truck for a sports car. "Hop in! We're heading to the city in style!"

The cousins arrived in Chicago right on Tuxedo's schedule. Bandanna stood in front of their high-class hotel, mesmerized by all the activity. Suddenly, he spotted someone driving off with their car. "Stop, thief!" Bandanna shouted as he chased after it. Tuxedo tried to stop him. "Get back here, Bandanna! It's just the valet! He's parking our car for us!" Bandanna stopped in his tracks, feeling foolish. "Sorry! My bad!"

Bandanna hoped they would take in a Cubs game at Wrigley Field. Instead, Tuxedo dragged Bandanna into every chic boutique on the Magnificent Mile. But when Tuxedo was busy shopping, a bored-to-the-bones Bandanna slipped out of the store. "Time for a little fun!" he giggled, and headed straight for the Sears Tower. Up the elevator he went, all the way to the skydeck on the 103rd floor. After taking in the view, down the elevator he went, pushing all the buttons as he left. Wearing a guilty grin, Bandanna made a quick exit before anyone could figure out what he had done.

When Tuxedo finally found Bandanna, he was playing his harmonica on Michigan Avenue. An admiring crowd was throwing change into his cowboy hat. "Stop making a spectacle of yourself!" Tuxedo scolded. Bandanna shrugged. "I'm just trying to have a little fun." Tuxedo pulled him away, much to the disappointment of the crowd. "Our next destination is the lively city that invented jazz. You can play your heart out there."

Tuxedo and Bandanna leaned out of their balcony and soaked up the sounds of New Orleans. Notes of lively jazz swirled in their ears. Bandanna wanted to dig right into the music of the French Quarter. But Tuxedo insisted they take a tour of historic homes in the Garden District. "Don't you just love the architecture?" Tuxedo sighed. "Once you've seen one old mansion you've seen them all," Bandanna muttered.

Tuxedo tried to liven things up. "Since we're in New Orleans, let's 'Laissez le bon temps rouler!'" Bandanna's face went blank. "Lazy what?" Tuxedo translated, "It means 'Let the good times roll'." Bandanna's face beamed like a street lamp on Bourbon Street. "Now you're talking my language!"

At the jazz club, Tuxedo snapped his fingers and tapped his toes to the catchy tunes. Bandanna pulled out his harmonica and jammed with the jazz musicians. Tuxedo cringed and waited for Bandanna to embarrass himself. But Bandanna brought down the house with his jazzy rendition of "When The Saints Go Marching In." A "Second Line Parade" formed and danced around the club's courtyard until the wee hours.

The next morning, Bandanna's head throbbed from too much music and he was woozy from staying up too late. "I guess it really is possible to have too much of a good thing! I need a vacation from our vacation!"

"I know just the place," Tuxedo replied. "A resort town on the coast of Florida."

The cousins toured the shore in their convertible. Palm trees swayed in the tropical breeze. Rows of ritzy resorts lined posh Palm Beach like diamonds on a tiara. "Welcome to the vacation destination of the rich and famous," Tuxedo announced.

That afternoon, they window-shopped on Worth Avenue and lunched at an outdoor café. "This touring is getting boring!" Bandanna complained over his meal. "Let's get to our resort and chill out."

Bandanna admired the view from the balcony in their oceanfront room. He quickly grabbed his boogie board. "Dude! Let's catch some waves!"

"Absolutely not," Tuxedo argued. "I'd hate to get my fur covered with gritty sand. Besides, the pool is *the* place to be seen."

"Geronimo!" Bandanna shouted as he launched into a tidal-wave-producing belly flop. Waves sloshed over the sides of the pool, soaking angry sunbathers. Bandanna tried to apologize. "Sorry! That's usually a big hit at the watering hole back home."

Bandanna crawled out of the pool, marched over to Tuxedo's lounge and read him the riot act. "This resort is too fancy and formal! I need to get down to earth and back to nature. Tomorrow we're exploring a national park in southern Florida. And I won't take no for an answer!"

Muggy mist gave a mysterious look to the swamps of the Everglades National Park. Bandanna and Tuxedo paddled their canoe through the Wilderness Waterway. Egrets tiptoed through tall grasses. Dragonflies droned in the hot and humid air. And mosquitos buzzed in Tuxedo's ears. He began scratching like a dog with fleas. "I'm being eaten alive!" he growled.

"Sorry, Tux. Guess I forgot to mention that The Everglades are home to forty-three kinds of mosquitoes. Try some of this citronella. It's mosquito kryptonite!"

The citronella repelled the pests and restored peace and quiet...until Tuxedo's phone began ringing to the tune of "New York, New York." Bandanna's blood boiled when Tux answered it.

"Tuxedo Teddy here. Tickets to the ballet? Fabulous! Let me check my calendar and..." He let out a horrified gasp as Bandanna grabbed the phone and tossed it into the swamp! Tuxedo leaned over and caught the phone just before it ended up in the snapping jaws of a hungry alligator.

"That's the last straw! Battling the elements in the backwoods is not my idea of a vacation!" Tuxedo proclaimed. "I'm departing for Philadelphia for a little culture and history. Farewell, Bandanna!"

"Well, touring boring cities isn't *my* idea of a vacation! I'm taking off for the Amish farms of Lancaster, Pennsylvania, for some simple country living. See ya later, alligator!" Bandanna snapped back.

"Let freedom ring!" the Liberty Bell seemed to echo. "Thank goodness Bandanna isn't here," Tuxedo thought. "He'd probably try to ring it!"

Walking the cobblestone streets of Philadelphia, Tuxedo felt as if he were back in the colonial era. He could imagine the founders of our country drafting documents of liberty in Independence Hall. Goosebumps formed under his fur when he viewed the original Constitution.

But the colonial horse-and-carriage ride seemed dull without Bandanna's lively banter. The old-fashioned dinner at the quaint restaurant seemed bland without Bandanna's gusto for good food. And the fife and drum corps just wasn't the same without Bandanna getting into the act. Tuxedo began to miss his good friend. "Bandanna is more than just a friend and a cousin. He's like a brother to me. And here I am in the 'city of brotherly love' without him." Tuxedo realized he couldn't enjoy the rest of the trip without Bandanna. He had to find him and finish their tour together.

Bandanna awakened to the tune of a crowing rooster. Life on the Amish farm began at dawn, but Bandanna didn't mind. "Good thing Tux isn't here," he thought. "He'd be as angry as a hive of hornets if he were woken up this early."

Helping with outdoor chores made Bandanna feel at one with nature. The Amish family ran the farm without any electricity or machinery. All the work was done by hand or with the help of horses.

But the family-style dinners seemed too quiet without Tuxedo's witty conversation. The bumpy horse-and-buggy rides were boring without Tuxedo's cranky complaints. And going to town just wasn't the same without Tuxedo stopping in every shop. Bandanna knew he couldn't enjoy the rest of his trip without his cousin. "I sure wish Tuxedo were here with me right now," Bandanna sighed.

Just then, his wish came true. "Yoo Hoo!" Tuxedo called, pulling up to the farm in a fancy sports car. The cousins greeted each other with apologies and big bear hugs. "Tomorrow we'll finish our tour together!"

Tuxedo and Bandanna plunged their paws into the white-capped waves of the Atlantic. "The Pacific marked the beginning of our tour. Reaching the Atlantic finally marks the end." Tuxedo announced.

"We've done it!" Bandanna declared. "We have truly traveled America the Beautiful 'from sea to shining sea'!"

They strolled the quiet Long Island beach. "When we were apart, I realized how much I enjoyed everything we shared. Canoeing, mule riding and camping really did add excitement and adventure to our tour," Tuxedo confided. "And if it weren't for you, I never would have toured a city or played in a jazz club. You really did add class and culture to our trip," Bandanna admitted. "We sure are different, but our differences turned our tour into a journey of discovery."

Bandanna suggested they spend the morning surfing. Tux wasn't very good at it, but when he wiped out, he just laughed. In the afternoon they toured the Montauk Lighthouse as Tuxedo proposed. Bandanna didn't enjoy all the history in the tour, but he loved climbing to the top of the lighthouse tower.

Tuxedo was still trying to catch his breath from the climb when his cell phone rang. "I have to get this. It's the President!" Bandanna's jaw dropped. "Mr. President? You've heard about our tour? Lunch at the White House? We'd be delighted!" Tuxedo hung up and grinned. "It looks like our trip isn't over yet!"

An official motorcade whisked Bandanna and Tuxedo past the magnificent monuments and museums of Washington, D.C. When they arrived at the White House, they were escorted to the Oval Office, where the President greeted them.

The President was very impressed with all he heard about the cousins' tour of the United States. "I hereby appoint Bandanna Bear 'Head Ranger of National Parks' and Tuxedo Teddy 'Honorary Historian of American Cities.' It will be your job to encourage all Americans to tour and explore our national parks and historic cities. It's up to you to see that these national treasures are protected and enjoyed." Bandanna and Tuxedo thanked the President and accepted their new positions with pride.

Before they left the nation's capital, the cousins visited the Lincoln Memorial, the Washington Monument and the Capitol Building. They even squeezed in a visit with the great granddaddy of all teddy bears—the original American teddy bear who resides in the Smithsonian Institution's Museum of American History!

The next day was the Fourth of July. Bandanna and Tuxedo set off for New York City to celebrate America's birthday with Lady Liberty.

Sailing on a ship in New York Harbor, Tuxedo and Bandanna gazed in wonder at the Independence Day fireworks. They looked like thunderstorms of glitter bursting in the black velvet sky. Sparks showered the New York City skyline like confetti. The fireworks were bright, but the Statue of Liberty's light of freedom and friendship burned brighter.

Tuxedo and Bandanna reflected on their
tour of the USA. Tuxedo summed up their
experiences rather eloquently. "The
American landscape is as diverse
as the Americans who call it home."
Bandanna put it another way. "America is
like a beautiful patchwork quilt, filled with
color and contrast." Together they cheered,
"Hooray for the USA!"

# America the Beautiful!
## Land That We Love